THOSE MAYBES'

ZAHID ASHRAF

NOTION PRESS

NOTION PRESS
India. Singapore. Malaysia.
ISBN xxx-x-xxxxx-xx-x

Disclaimer

This anthology is a work of fiction. It contains write-ups from various writers. We guided them to not to use any copyrighted contents. The compiler has tried his best to use original content from co-authors. But if there is any mistake, we won't be liable for it.

<u>*Acknowledgments*</u>

This anthology was not possible without the help of our co-authors. Each and every co-author has put his/her best efforts for this anthology. Thanks to the publisher to support this anthology at every stage. This anthology is compiled by Zahid Ashraf and managed by Sahil Chopra.

Efforts aren't only made by the compiler but every co-author has helped to complete this anthology in the best possible way.

THOSE MAYBES'

Zahid Ashraf

Freelance writer, Poet, Voracious reader and a
Motivational speaker.

Zahid Ashraf, A 21 years old Bpharm pursuing student
at GCOP Aba'd Maharashtra was born and raised in
Sopore (A town in Baramulla North Kashmir), but his
nomadic inclinations made him encamp in New Delhi,
Chandigarh, Mumbai, Pune, Aurangabad, Mohali,
Amritsar, Haryana and Kashmir, where he currently
lives with his family.
He turned to writing in 2014 as a novice and now is an
ardent writer. He has inspired many by his poetry, prose,
short stories, tales, words of courage, the power of love,
feelings and emotions etc.
Now he wants to create a name for himself in the world
of fiction.

To connect with him.
Follow him on Instagram @zahid__ashraf Email :
stillunknown112@gmail.com
"Bikhair Detay Hai Insan Ko Kuch Halaat Zindagi Kay..

Har Bikhra Hua Shaks Ishq Mai Nahi Bikharta.."

"Sajde"

"Laazmi hai ibaadat mein dil ka bhi jhukna, Mehaz sar k
jhukaane ko sajda nahi kehte"

Ye kya hai mje sajde mein sukoon kyu nahi mil raha,
Mera dil kyun bechain hai har waqt

Mai sajda tou kar raha hu lekin bandagi kyun nahi hai,
dil mutmayin kyun nahi hai

Mere Rab ka tou waada hai Sajde mein mujhe pavoge
Mere Rab ka tou waada hai, tum sajda karo hal bhi nikal
aayega

In sajdoon ki qubooliyat ka waada hota hai haqeekatan

Aur Waada hai humse hamare Rab ka,
Tum Duaa ko haath uthavoge Vo khaali nahi bejega

Kyun phir duniya k ahbab mein kho se gaya hai hum,
Kyun bas sajda ada karne ko ibaadat samaj baithay hai

Dil ka sukoon bhi hamesha talaashte rahe ahbab mein,
Kbi sajdoon mein bhi talaasha hota, mil hi jata

Aur hal bhi nikal aayega gar ho dil ka sajda,
Niyat saaf nahi hoti mehaz saja kar nishan-e-sajda

Nateeje bhi niyatoon pe milte hai sajdoon ki banawat pe
nahi, Gar Ho dil mein bandagi tou pavoge sajde mein
Khuda ko

"Haan Laazmi hai ibaadat mein dil ka bhi jhukna, Mehaz
sar k jhukaane ko sajda nahi kehte.."
-Zahid Ashraf

ZAHID ASHRAF

"Kashmir"

"Kashmir ke faisle ka hak, Sirf kashmir ke logun ka hai"

Koii ahl-e-sitam se ye jaa ke batlaye,
Kashmir ke faisle ka hak sirf Kashmir ke logun ka hai

Jo Kashmir ko tod kar banana chahte thay Hindustan,
Jamia aur Assam ko bhi kar gaye vo khoon-e-saar

Baat bas Kashmir ki nahi rahi ab, Ye inka dastoor bhi
sahi nahi ab

Aaye thay ye adakari se badalne Kashmir,
Ban raha hai inki wajah se Hindustan bhi Kashmir

Na inme saleeqa hai na hi insaniyat,
Bane rahe hai masoomun ka khoon bahaake jumhuriyat

Awaaz na uthavoge tou tum bhi inme shamil, Saath na
doge hamara tou tum bhi ek qaatil

Karte gaye vo zulum, hum darguzar karte gaye Karte
gaye vo sitam hum hosla rakhte gaye

Jis din sabr ki inteha hogi ye jaan lena,
Bardasht ka hukum humko bhi nahi ye yaad rakh lena

Haan bhule nahi vo zulm jo kiya gaya humpar, Haan
bhule nahi vo jabr jo kiya gaya humpar

Nahi bhulenge hum ye sab yaad rakha jayega, saare
shaheedoon ka badla liya jayega

Ye Kashmir hamara hai,
Yahaan ka faisla bhi hum hi karinge

Kyunki Kashmir k faisle ka hak sirf Kashmir ke logun
ka hai, sirf Kashmir ke logun ka hai

"Koii ahl-e-sitam se ye jaa ke batlaye,
Kashmir ke faisle ka hak sirf Kashmir ke logun ka hai.."
-Zahid Ashraf

"Unhe ishq kisi aur se tha"

Vo intezar karate gaye, Hum intezar karte gaye

Vo sapne dikhate gaye, Hum sapne dekhte gaye

Vo jhoot bolte gaye, Hum aitibaar karte gaye

Vo kabhi mazak, kabhi tamasha banate gaye, Hum
Kabhi mazak, kabhi tamasha bante gaye

Vo dard dete gaye, Hum dard sehte gaye

Najane kyun unki dil ki baatein humse anjaan rahi

Vo kabhi aaye, tou kabhi gaye,
Humne kabhi koyi shikwa na shikayat ki unse

Vo tou kisi aur se mohabbat karte thay, Aur hum unse
mohabbat karte thay

Vo kisi aur k liye jeete thay, Aur hum unke liye jeete
thay

Vo kisi aur k liye roz-o-shab rote thay, Aur hum unke
liye roz-o-shab rote thay

Unki duaa'en kisi aur k liye hoti thi, Aur hamari duaa'en unke liye hoti thi

Unhune jo bhi kiya, humein na koyi gila hai unse na hi koyi nafrat

Jaise hum unke liye tadapte thay,
Waise hi tou vo kisi aur k liye tadapte thay

Unki na thi khataa koyi,
Vo tou khud fanaah k safar k thay

Bas aakhir mein yun hua,
mohabbat na unhe mili aur na hi humein..

-Zahid Ashraf

"Ishq ko ishq keh dene se ishq nahi hai hota"

Ishq ko zubaan ki zaroorat nahi padti, ishq tou mehsoos hai hota, Ishq ko bas keh dene se ishq nahi hai hota

Khabar nahi hui humko bhi ki ishq kab hai hua Ishq ko bas keh dene se ishq nahi hai hota

Maloom thi har baat unki humein, phir bhi hamesha humne suna, kyunki Ishq ko bas keh dene se ishq nahi hai hota

Suna tou gaya tha mujhe, kaash samja bhi gaya hota, ishq ko bas ishq keh dene se ishq nahi hai hota

Yaad nahi aate vo, lekin unhe bhulaya bhi nahi jata, Ishq ko bas keh dene se ishq nahi hai hota

Sambhal gaya hai dil agar tou dobara ishq kyu nahi hota,
Ishq ko bas keh dene se ishq tou nahi hai hota

Kab thi manzoor humein kisi ki shirkat ishq mein, phir
bhi humne kabhi aah bhi na kiya, kyunki ishq ko bas
ishq keh dene se ishq tou nahi hai hota

Sukoon tou hamesha kehne se zyada rone se mila, ishq
ko ishq keh dene se ishq nahi hai hota

Sabr ka kaam hai ishq, jitna bhi bole phir bhi na hoga
kabhi humse bayaan, Ishq ko bas keh dene se ishq nahi
hai hota

Agaz-e-mohabbat se anjam-e-mohabbat tak sab hai
jaante ki dil hai toodna,
phir bhi mohabbat ki, kyunki bas ishq ko ishq keh dene
se ishq tou nahi hai hota

"Ki hai mohabbat 'Zahid' , ho ek ya do tarfa, ab sabr bhi
rakh, nibhana bhi seekh jaa.. Mehaz ishq ko ishq keh
dene se ishq tou nahi hai hota.."
-Zahid Ashraf

"Aur uss din"

'Aur uss din usne kaha tha usse mohabbat hai humse'

Abi bhi yaad hai humein vo din, jis din usne kaha tha
usse mohabbat hai humse.. Kash ki ye din bhi wohi din
hota, jis din usne kaha tha usse mohabbat hai humse

Hota hamare bas mein tou waqt ko bhi rok dete , Uss ek
din mein saari Zindagi bita dete, jis din usne kaha tha
usse mohabbat hai humse

Uthaya bhi na gayi nigaah kisi aur k janeb, uss ek din se
jis din usne kaha tha usse mohabbat hai humse

Aata gaya vo khayalun mein musalsal, Unki mohabbat
mein bhi qaid se hoke reh gaye thay hum, uss ek din se
jis din usne kaha tha usse mohabbat hai humse

Sajde bhi kiye humne, Mannate bhi maangi humne, Phir
bhi na jane kya reh gaya tha

Vo ek din jo tha, uss ek din k baad hai har raat ki yahi
kahaani,
har raat dil ka tadapna, Phir kuch bechain hona, phir teri
justujuu mein rona

Gar mohabbat nahi thi unhe, phir bhi kyu kaha
unhune,Ye sawaal kar Nahi paraha, uss ek din se jis din
usne kaha tha usse mohabbat hai humse

Bhale hi tha sab fareb uss din ka, thi mohabbat bhi jhooti
hi sahi uss din ki,
Phir bhi dil khush tha uss ek din se jis din usne kaha tha
usse mohabbat hai humse

Maana dikhawa hi sahi, adakaar hi sahi, matlabi hi sahi,
Phir bhi dil ko koyi malaal nahi unse, uss ek din ka jis
din usne kaha tha usse mohabbat hai humse

Ab iss dil ka tadapna, tadapkar sambhalna, sambhal kar
ye kehna, Mohabbat hai unse, rahegi hamesha

Manzil hamari wohi thi hamesha, Shayad hi mohabbat
ab hogi dobara

Iss dil ki kahaani sunayi muqammal, Magar safar hamara
adhura reh gaya tha

Ye keh kar choda unhune humein, ki mohabbat nahi thi
uss ek din bhi jis din kaha tha mohabbat hai tumse

Kaash ki ishq hona hamare bas mein hota, Kaash ki vo
din kabhi aaya hi na hota

Uss ek din k baad har din hu khudko dhoondta, Kaash ki
vo din kabhi aaya hi na hota

Nahi mil raha hu khudko, khudse hu kahin dhoor jaa
basa, Kaash ki vo din kabhi aaya hi na hota
-Zahid Ashraf

"Baat dil ki thi"

Thi mohabbat humein unse, ya tha bas ye ek fasana, sab
baat dil ki thi

Tha koyi shor mere andar, ya mai kuch toot raha tha, sab
baat dil ki thi

Tha jaanna ye bohat zaroori k kis janeb chal diye hai
hum, kyunki baat dil ki thi

Mila hai mere andar hi mujhe kuch mujme,
Jaan liya hai iss safar mein khudko maine, kyunki baat
dil ki thi
Tha vo ishq-e-mamnu, ye baat pehle se thay jaante,
Phir bhi hua kuch taasiir-e-ishq humpe, kyunki baat dil
ki thi

Mohabbat bhi hui thi unse, jo thay pehle se kisi aur k, ab
dekh kar kya dil lagate, jab baat dil ki thi

Hua bhi tou vo kisi aur ka jana, nahi thay hum unke
jabhi bhi, ye baat maani nahi gayi humse, kyunki baat dil
ki thi

Vo sabr ki inteha jana, Vo dil ka tadapna jana, Mohabbat
mein jab dil toota, tou toot kar bhi chalna pada, kyunki
baat dil ki thi

Aata humko bhi unse berukhi se pesh aana, lekin kiya
nahi gaya aisa kabhi humse, kyunki baat dil ki thi

Hua jo bhi tabse, kiya jo bhi tabse, kaha jo bhi tabse,
phir bhi mohabbat unhi se thi hamesha, kyunki baat dil
ki thi

Iss dil ki baat mein sab kuch seh liya humne, kaash ki iss
dil ki baat nahi hoti, kaash ki mohabbat na hui hoti

Haan thi vo mohabbat ab samja, nahi tha vo koyi fasana,
tha shor bhi mere andar, mai toot bhi raha tha

"Iss ishq k safar mein 'Zahid' , itna tou fayida hua
hamara.. Ki dil lagake tumse khudme safar kiya maine.."
-Zahid Ashraf

Tyba idrees

I'm tyba idrees, village girl from Kashmir. I'm 16 and I'm a medical student.

The moon died in my arms, unleashing my disgrace,
I didn't thought of a dirge, ephemeral death in my space.
I wished, wish to visit my heaven back in my very own
town, An exhort, I heard from graveyards, got me upside
down.
People finding hope in me and I being hapless though,
In the inexorable situation, where a piece of mine was
still kept so. Why did I lost the flavours of saffron,
despite my will,
Time and again autumn was my survival, then why
wasn't I still. Alive, is a heavy word, just breathing the
life of a reprieve,
Oh my mad heart be brave, a lot of sins you got to
deprive. Tyba ∞

An aberration that I myself have went through,
Or the never ending contusion that was made by you! Or
the curse that you made in dearth for cupidity,
In a verse of defunct book, I presumed it as humility. An
elegy, I wrote on my gravestone for your enervate,
In my ephemeral life, a fortuitous ending that I dedicate.
Or the impute that my invective curse has given to you,
To the noxious obdurate that you did, therefore I'll do it
too. As paradigm I stand, in a world of solicitous
solitude,
With my pen ,bleeding ink to highlight your turpitude.
No more injustice.
— Tyba!

Love without tranquility, is like tear in an eye, We
address the testimony, but don't resist to cry !
& so shall I, will figure out every path of clamour, Being
the reasons of times or an adverted spectator ! Hope
without transom, is like a library without books , We
sedate ourselves but cannot mark the hooks !

THOSE MAYBES'

And so shall I , make every wise verse a doctrine, Being
the promise of a nomad or a sour turpentine !
Tyba

<u>Adeeba Feroz Shah</u>

Adeeba is a 13 year old girl from srinagar kashmir. She is Youngest writer and poetess of kashmir..she loves writing.and she writes poems , books and articles..She at a very delicate and innocent age found her destines in the vessels of poetry.

"Verily the darkness of judgements can never surpass
my perseverance for I have stardust running in my veins,
even if all the evils will cast their shadows over me. I
will scintillate from within".
~*Adeeba Feroz Shah*

"When you will be near to success, you will face many
people who will be filled with pessimism, stay enough
brawny to face them".
~*Adeeba Feroz Shah*

MY DAD! MY EVERTHING!

Whenever i see u my heart is filled with joy and love,
Whenever i not see you my heart goes numb
You are the one who will never hurt me,
You are the one who will never stop to enchant me You
are the one who will love me unconditionally, You are
the one who natured me
U are very important and special person in my life You
are my life, My DAD!
You are the beat to my heart..
I LOVE U TO THE MOON AND BACK! MY DAD!
LIVE LONG♡♤♧
PENNED DOWN BY
~*Adeeba Feroz Shah*

<u>Tasaduq Qayoom Shah</u>

Tasaduq Qayoom Shah was born in Kashmir in April 1994.He had his initial schooling from I.E.I Badipora Chadoora. He moved to Maulana Azad national Urdu university when he was 20 , to study Urdu literature at the university of Hyderabad. He has worked as a teacher at Aglow Educational Institute Chadoora and has written for various publications including "The Creative Minds" where he was CO-Author. He has also authorized a book "ASHK VA ISHQ" .He is currently based in Kashmir. He loves observing people in streets, parks, cafes as well, where he often searches for their thoughts. He has a secret list of hundred wishes, which he want to fulfill in this one lifetime.
You can connect with him on Instagram as bismil-writer or on Twitter as bismil-writer.

1. Merai Aangan Mai Terai Naam Ki Awaazain Kab
Goonjai Gi
Merai Kamrai Mai Terai Padai Baal Mai Kab Uthaavo
Ga 2.Haara Huva Lauta Hoon Uski Mehfil Sai Mai Aaj
Khairiyat Poocho Gai Too Khudkashi Karo Ga 3.Aab
Terai Naam Ki Virid Karta Phirta Hoon Mai
Aab Shahr Walai Mujai Majnoon Keh Kai Bhulatai Hai
4.Meri Zaat Mai Tum Kab Sai Zam Huvi Ho
Merai Dil Nai Tumhai Badshah Kab Bana Diya

1. Mai Iss Tarah Uski Yaad Mai Jal Raha Hoon
Jiss Tarah Aatish E Namrood Jal Utha Tha
2.   Talab Uski Aab Shidat Mai Tabdeel Huvi Hai
Bismil Usnai Aanai Ka Waadah Jo Aaj Barsoo Baid Taal
Diya
3.   Woh Baatoon Mai Allah Hafiz Kahai Too

Mujai Har Taraf Judayii Ki Bo Aati Hai
4.   Terai Hukum Sai Hoo Chalai Too Jannat Sai
Laut Aavo Ga
Terai Roothnai Ka Agar Kaho Yea Kamaal Sanam Kaafi
Hai

1.   Woh Hai Ki Meri Jaan Lainai Pai Tulai Huvai
Hai
Mai Hoon Ki Uskai Shahr Mai Panah Laikai Baitha Hoo
2.   Iss Aarzii Tasveer Ka Kya Kar Loogai Merai
Sanam
Dil Ko Kuredh Kar Tasver Bana Kai Dikhaoo Ga
3.   Chaloo Aankh Band Karloon Mai, Kuch Mudat
Kai Liyay
Taaki Tumhai Khawaab Mai Daikhnai Ka Tajruba Hasil
Ho
4.   Halak Sai Kuch Nahi Utarta,Saans Zara Sii
Rukk Jati Hai

Yea Halat Uss Waqt Ki Hoti Hai, Jab Tuu Rooth Kai
Chali Jaati Hai

1.	Jaam I Maurifat Pilla Kai Mujai
Merai Dil Ko Kistarah Sataanai Lagai
2.	Yea Kis Qissai Ko Mukhtasar Kar

Rahai Ho Zalim
Yea Koie Afsaana Nahi,Ishq Kiya Hai Mainai
3.	Ek Adad Dil Ka Kaat Liya Warna Sara Dil Bai
Wafaie Ki Zad Mai Aata
4.	Teri Shahr Ki Barsaar Ka Kya Kaho Mai Meri
Aankhoon Ko Haraa Daitii Hai....
5.	Bai Suud Thi Unki Bataain Aur Khan Unmai
Dam Tha
Ham Nai Bhii Laakh Samjaana Chaaha Mager Zaida
Kuch Kam Hai"

Rubaii

1. Nikal Kai Jannat Sai Koie Hoor Aayi Hai Saath Apnai
Chand Firishtai Laayi Hai
Kya Hamsai Unhai Mohabat Bantii Nahi Thi
Ki Aap Nai Sardaar Bhii Woh Saath Laayay Hai 2.Mai
Lipat Kai Na Rooloo Koie Rook Loo Mujai Woh Kayi
Baar Apnai Sai Hata Chuki Hai Mujai Shayad Kaat
Loon Mai Poori Umar Uskai Bagair
Yehi Wadah Apnai Dil Sai Kiyay Mager Woh Sata Rahi
Hai

Adna mehraj

Nobody was my support. You have to support yourself and i think that is the beauty of being a woman.

1)   zara yaad kr merai hamsafar Kisai pyar tha terai naam sai Kisai pyar tha terai kaam sai Kisai pyar tha teri zaat sai Kisai pyar tha teri baat sai Kisai pyar tha teri hassi sai Kisai pyar tha terai ghamo sai Ae Adna ab toh thehar jaa Usai farq nhi pdta terai honai Ya na honai sai!!

2)   zara ruk zindagi thoda sabar toh kr Mera hamsafar abhi aaya nhi is mnzil pr
Hogayai hai ham juda tohmatu kai rah guzar par.. Usai keh aaj b tera haq hai meri har sham par!!

3)   hova youn ki mohabbat hogayi Hova youn ki zindagi badal gayi
Hova youn ki mohabbat nafratu mai badal gyi.. Dil nai phir ye gawahi di Adna
Akhir toh akelai pad hi gayi!

4)   hum aisai na thai kabhi Jaisa apnai banadiya..
Hum nai jhooth b kaha t Apnai sach manliya
Baroosa na ho agar hamara Merai dil sai poch apnai hamai Kitna kafir krdiya!!

1Meethi meethi baatai kr kai log Zindagi ko veeran banadaitai hai..

2)   mujai jo b mila, jab b mila
Jaisa b mila apnai mtlb ka bhoka hi kue mila!!

3)   waqt bai waqt halatu nai shikaadi Hoshyari wrna..
Ham b masoomiyat ki had tak masoom thai..

4)   na koi kasam kr na koi reham kr
Bass dikhaava kr chod, chain sai bewafai kr

5)   Ab nahi rakhtai umeedai wafa kisai sai..
Be_raham log hai dil tod daiatai hai!!

6)   libas jaisai hogayai hai log Ik oodha, ik choda

7)   mohabbat krnai mai sab ustaad Nikah ka bolo toh sab bai _bass

8)   kamyabi par choomnai walai Takleefo mai hath chudalaitai hai

9)   hum hmesha wafa par kayam rahaigai Par mohabbat chod di !!
10)   mainai apnai kirdaar ko kabhi girnai na diya Dokhai toh bohat khayai pr kabhi doka na diya!!
11)   ye sachai hai itefaaq nhi Ham jaisa hona koi mazaaq nhi!!

mera dil aayinai ki tarah hai Tumhara dil aisa hai kya..
mai ik khali kitaab ho tum bar sakhtai ho kya.. mai bewafayoun sai nazrai nhi milati
Tum wafadar bansaktai ho kya Mai mohabat mai marsakti ho
Tum aise mohabbat krsaktai ho kya!!
2)   hum nai jisko pyar sikhaaya vo hamai bai wafa samj kr chod gaya Ham nai jisko izzat di
Vo hamai gira hova samj kr chod gaya Hum jiskai marhaam banai
Vo hamai zakham daikar chod gaya
Sari umar wafa kai rastai par chalti rahi adna.. Par ham nai jisko rasta diya vo
Hamai beech rastai par chod gaya!!
3)   jab ehsaas khatam Ehmiyat khatam Izaat khatam Mohabbat khatam Toh samj lejiyai Mohabbat khatam!!
4)   har sath mustakil nahi rehta Har pyar pora nhi hota..
Reh jati hai kuch adhoori khwaahisai Har shaks wafadaar nhi hota!!

Zainab yousuf

I am reader which makes me a passionate writer.I use my canvas as mirror and draw my heart out on it.When a writer meets an artist that makes him/her a perfect interactor hence,that's what i am.
Pursuing B.A honor's

THOSE MAYBES'

Should I speak up?
Should I speak up?
How they Wrecked my life. Should I speak up?
How they torn my clothes with knife.

I am yelling can anyone hear. They're still free without
any fear. They mangled me as if I was a paper.
Then whanged me away as if I was a wrapper.

Their eyes were full of lust.
They smoulder my dignity to the dust. They left my
body with so many scars.
Then caged my soul in the wake of the bars.

Should I speak up?
How they auctioned my soul. Should I speak up?
How they demolished my every goal.

Should I speak up?
How they Wrecked my life. Should I speak up?
How they torn my clothes with knife.

"And then they caged her in the darkness of
ignorance.As if she was a dead body caged inside the
coffin".

The lost battle The love she thought. The lust that was.
The care she thought. The compassion that was.
The battle of love she was loosing now.

The wings she thought. The cage that was.
The blessing she thought. The curse that was.
The battle of love she was loosing now.

The light she thought. The darkness that was. The bliss
she thought. The suffering that was.
The battle of love she was loosing now.

The heaven she thought. The hell that was.
The sunshine she thought. The cloud he was.
The battle of love she was loosing now.

The warmth she thought. The cold he was.
The life she thought.
The death that was.
The battle of love then she lost.

Zalimo k jabar ki intiha hogayi Humare b sabar ki intiha
hogayi.
Laakh roke yeh humko hum na ruken gai Azaadi ki iss
jung mein hum na jukein gai. Lehrana woh parcham
khawab hain humara
Lena azaad hawa mein saans khawab hain humara.
Rokna ab humko tou mumkin nhi
Khushiyan hum b manayen gai aj nhi tou kal hi sahi.

Yun beintiha tadpana koi apsai seekhai
Mohabbat Ko humari baar baar thukrana koi apsai
seekhai Hum parwana ban k jal gaye apki aag mein
"kisi aur k lia jal gayi khe kar"tuhmat lagana koi apsai
seekhai.

Humein mohabbat kar k bagawat mili Aur unhain
bagawat kar k mohabbat Samjh nhi aata sahib!
Yeh humari badnaseebi hai
Ya hum unki khushnaseebi ban gaye.

Dil janta tha woh bewafa hain Lekin uff!yeh kambakht
Rok na paya khud ko unsai wafayen karne se.

Nadim Masroor

Hailing from Gundpora Rampora Bandipora.Doing B.a

(1) Oh my dad!
When this dark sun is bright ,oh my dad! I am waiting
day and night ,ohh my dad!

Every corner ,full of choas, in my home... Come and set
,things right ,oh my dad!

Whom you gave to ,ur pigeons to be nourished... On our
flesh ,now they bite,oh my dad!

In these blowing winds; cutting theards off. I am running
chopped kite,oh my dad!

I am scared of this crowd ;talking loud.. Want to hold
your finger tight,oh my dad!

Tell me without climbing your shoulders . How can I
touch any height ,oh my dad!

It was only you ,who could tell me better. What is wrong
,what is right,oh my dad!

Now fight alone ,pray for him,oh nadim! Stop chanting
in every plight ,oh my dad!

(2) He's changed a lot.
Believe me or not ,he's changed a lot.
What has changed in him, I'm going to jott... Once was a
time ,cowardice was a crime.
My youth was in fervor ,my youth was in prime ; The
sole weapon he used to have.
He had no penny but he was brave . Was ready to
confrort any kinda wave;
Whether it was a jail or it ws a grave...

Now !! his sister is dead shot ,and he is on the cot. He's
watching tv shows, he's having wine tot.
His veins carry water and blood is not hot. Is listening
cool songs oh! lend him a pot.

Urdu Gazal

Uspar rehbar khud bhi gumrah hota hai.. Koi rasta aisa
rasta hota hai...
Uski zulfoun key jangal main roazaana.. Kaaley
saanpoun kaa ek pehra hota hai.

Teri yaadein saathi banti hai jab bhi. Tanhaayi ka mujh
pai hamla hota hai.

Roothi hoti hai us sai parchaayi bhi.. Koi koi itna tanha
hota hai...

Terey aaney ki afwahh sun'ney key baad .. Koan tere
aaney tak zinda hota hai..

Tum kya jaano is jumley ka kya matlab? Qatraa qatraa
mil kar dariya hota hai.

Iss sey zyada kya teazi ho tarqi main.. Bacha bachpan
mai hi booda hota hai.

Syed Sohaib Aijaz

Assalaamualaikum,
"My name's Sohaib Aijaz and I am here to flow,
With someone who would let me grow. Let me pierce the cloud
And play the role of Navvy, Trust me when i say,
Am simply here "to savvy"!."

"Madrugada"

Madrugada... I AM still alive.

A caffeine nap to blow up my mind.
Rendered to a corner the World lives through his sight.
Doesn't give a damn what's outside the hive,
If poked needlessly...he shows his might. People came
by,chattered in a disgraceful way,
Coerced him to the edge,that drops in a peaceful bay.

Once drowned, there's his will that let him breath.
Alas!,they made certain no bubbles pops up to its
wreath. Though the storm bide...he threw the vessel and
ran.
Reuniting the whole he dangles and cried-
"I witnessed the thread between a man and a tree". He
widens the lid and murmured to thee.

Searched for it an ETERNITY went by, a set of
connections we all seek but die. Those were the
intentions,
the whole gave to all.
As the 'All' was the tree, and the 'whole' was all.

There was a man envisioned as he leaves the vessel. He
looked up to him and the heavens drizzled. "Truth was
ahead we thrive not to see".
He glitched his breath to talk to thee-
"There's something I'd like to say as I tried to recall..." A
lightning struck that baffled them all.

As the light was gone and darkness lusted,
He reckoned the words that he most trusted...- "He didn't
planned to live,
he didn't planned to die. He stood over there by, seeing
all this was a lie."

"I am confused"

I am confused, Trust me i am. I am alone,
Rather i am separated.
I am the target placed at a place. So that,
I should get resolved with a peaceful pace. I was born!...
Was that a sentence?. Lived for a day,
died in repentance.
Went through the process, learned to lie.
Enjoyed the moment, Then got denied.
I laughed I laughed I cried I cried.
To make things upright, Though they weren't right.
Well!...
Here's to the moment i never spent, My heart ached,
As I beared no dent.

Shazia Masood

"Many years ago, I met a lady who shared her pain and grief with me and wished if she could meet a person who could write her pain so that all the ladies in the world could read it and get a lesson from it.
Her pain left me in a state of restlessness and I start writing.
That day was the beginning of my writing. Since, then writing is my passion. I set forth, what I observe in society. I tell the untold stories".

"Everyone writes the story of red roses, but I write the story of withered ones."

Shazia Masood is a writer from Pulwama Kashmir. She is doing journalism and mass communication from GCW M.A ROAD Srinagar. "

The misunderstanding.

It melted down all their love
As the sun's heat melts ice, And faded away as the smell
of a withered rose. And the hatred continued,
dancing in their hearts And one day again they met
With their hearts buried in hatred And their cold hearts
Denying them for a talk.
Out of the corner of his eye, he noticed The antimony in
her eyes
And her baby pink lips With her blushing cheeks And
the shining eyes
with a small tear at her eye corner He was trying to say
something
But before he Could say it. She left! He continued to see
her from the back The drooping black hair floating in air.
Like the pendulous branches of the weeping willow. He
continued to look at her
Till she disappeared in the crowd. And he repented on
his fate
For not giving him a chance. His fate offered him a
chance But he'd lost that opportunity Which comes just
at once.

A small town girl.

Diving in the air,
To have a feeling of a bird,
A Lamborghini, A trip to moon ,
A light dinner on the top of Eiffel Tower, Was just a
dream for her,
When she realised that She is a girl and That too a girl
from a small town.
Her whole world turned upside down For a movement
But she doesn't stop dreaming

She dreamed still high,Still big and still strong. And then
,
She finds hope in the rays of sun and the flash of light
that creep into her room through the window gap.
She started to find hope
in the nude and the lifeless tree after every fall of leaf
certain to get back its veins after every lifeless autumn.
She started to find hope in the finicky farmer who put
year round seed in the barren land and
get fields cherished with fruit.

A goodbye from the sun.

Looking at the sky i found, the moving clouds
and the flying birds twirling over my head
and the smooth touch of the leaves to my pinkish lips
and a beautiful butterfly searching for a black-eyed
susan in the same way
i was searching for him
with the movement of my eyes
i found the sun that was just above my head had now
cwtched the mountains
and was saying me good night and perhaps a good bye.
as the sun know me from decades and had seen me
troubling
at every move of my life. giving me a new hope
at every dawning of a new day but now the sun is itself
gloomy, dejected and dark,
worn to frazzle of being a witness to my failure after
failure.

<u>Sneha Kumari</u>

I was not the one i was acting like,
I never wanted to be the one i became like, I tried so
much to control myself,
But every night i found myself afraid, Like sitting in the
room corner,
I was watching myself changing from here to there, I
was rejected but was never answered,
I was never satisfied with any reason, All i was expected
to go on accepting, Accepting everything that was going
on,
Slowly somewhere i was trying to rebuilt me, Rebuilt in
a manner where I dont lose them, Them with whom i
always wanted to be with, And i lost them because of my
mistakes, Mistakes that i never realised i did,
And then when i had nothing to lose further, I found
myself as an unbreakable stone,
A stone who maintains itself as same, Whatever goes on
around doesnt matter,
I felt like i have burnt my feelings and affections to
ashes, But now also i want to thank everyone those who
criticised, Who left me alone in the battle to fight
myself,
For if they wouldn't had done that,
I would have never been at this point,
A point where i think i belong to everyone, But dont
want anyone to belong to me,
I am at a point of success where i have what i deserve..

Whenever tried something new in life,
Either was marked as imperfect or less efficient, Every
step when moved forward,
Taunts where what echoing in ears,
As if i dont know that i am just not perfect, Obviously i
am not like many others,
I might not be smart as another expects, I might not be
efficient as the next one,

Does it means i cant try to be one among others, If i dont
get what others talk in any sense,
If i have different point of views, How does it mean that
i m critising, Saying out my point of views,
I understood was discussing on something, Because i
never asked other to shut up, Acting like what i am,
Is like reveling myself and not being fake, How does it
offers an opportunity to judge, Backbitching against me
became a choice, But togetherness was never an award,
So alone even when one among crowd, How lonely it
makes me feel,
Should i give away my life because i know, I know i m
not capable and smart enough, So should i leave
everyone forever.

Was it really my fault you blamed me for, I was cursed
for spoiling our relation,
A relation which you had filled with lies, And over
several times you shouted,
You shouted with disgust to shut me up, But how did it
change the truth,
The truth you tried to hide away, Which you never
confessed,
For which you excused the fear of losing, Of which i
was awared by everyone but you, The person I wanted to
be with forever,
The one i trusted to be a piece of me,
I never reay anything could go wrong with, I dont know
if i was overconfident,
Or if the mistake i did being blind on you,
Did ever something happened like you felt as unknown,
You are stranger to me but we are not here alone,
I want to halt but i am being interrogated, Questioned of
how many times being fooled, And above all, shouldn't
had i done this, Had i done a blunder scratching the
truth,

Or should had just smiled at the funeral of my trust,
Would that have made our bond stronger, Vaccating me
from within,
Leaving the loyalty, the death song singing.

Rabia Gillani

I am Syeda Rabia Gillani from bandipora JK. By profession I am a social worker, from the past two years working with an NGO. I had develop the interest for literature at a very young age and then the hidden emotions of mine drive me to portray them on the paper so to express the unspoken me I started writing poetry.Till now I had write volumes of poetry and a few stories. The language I persuade more for write ups is Urdu but I had also written in Punjabi and English.

01
Kaheen fasaad e Jung o jadal hai Kaheen wabaoun ka
dour douraan hai

Hum aaj Kay muflis hain
Hmare naseeb kahan aman o amaan hai!

Tishnagi mei nawab hain hum Be-hissi Kay pasha bhi

K ab Kay humain ehsas ki aas nahi
K ab Kay humain qadroun ka pas kahan hai?

Bohat afsah huay hain hum aaj ki awam Afhaam se jinhe
sarokaar kahan hai!

Aqadeemah Kay aqaarib hua karte thai jo Aqaala! Aaj
woh musalman ghafil yahan hain

02
Mere zakham e jigar kay paemane mei Ab aasodagi bhi
baqi nahi

Main tan e tanha houn shaam o seher Ab mjhe hasrat e
qurb baqi nahi

Khalal hai kay ranjish, magar hai Ab pur hone ki
khawaish baqi nahi

Gidh hain meri laash Kay gird a gird Ab amaan ki Surat
e haal baqi nahi

Meri tishnagi pe khush hone wale Ab mjhe meh ki talab
baqi nahi

Roz e mehshar hongay hisab kay ma'mle Ab mjh mei
woh aag baqi nahi

Main bismil houn apne aashiyane mei Ab mjhe bisraam
ki chah baqi nahi

03
Aaj phir guzre ge ik raat qayamat ki
Aaj phir ik toufan mere sarhane barse ga Aaj phir
douhraei jaey ge batain hijar ki
Aaj phir mera zehn o qalb tamashe se guzre ga

Bholi nahi thi jisai main barsoun, woh chehra e jaanan
Aaj ki shaam nazroun se bar bar guzre ga

Lamha lamha ik tishnagi darkinaar kar Kay bhi Aaj ki
raat meh-kashi Kay bina he be-haal guzre ga

Mere qalb o jigar mei zalzale ka sa smaan hai Aaj ki raat
mera har peher rote rote guzre ga

Bewafae na uc ne ke, na meri wafa ka qasoor tha
Aaj shab e bedaari rahe GE, jagraata dil ko behlate guzre
ga

Qeher pe qeher, qayamat pe qayamat tou kat chuki hai
Aaj ki raat dil maidan e hashar, pul e siraat se guzre ga

Aansoyoun ki jhari bhi lagi rahe GE, firaq ka manzar
aam hoga Main bina ashk royoun ge Aysh lamha lamha
laho guzre ga

<u>Tahir Ahmad</u>

Tahir Ahmad form karnah tangdhar

ishQ Mae b sabar kii intihaa hOogayii Dil Mae unkii
Yaad beintihAa hOogayii

HAlat-e-nazaa Mae Aagaye saAkii had hOgayii.. VO
Aaye kYa fAeda ab tOo fAatihaa hOgayii

khuShiyAn bhii ab gham-e- zindagii hOgayii Tasalii hai
jaanE Mae rUuh rehaa hOogayii

Abii zinda hai bss Ek khabar hOogayii
HaaeY Marne se phlE khabar laa -intihAa hOogayii

KYa khUub Tahir gOoya ki ek Yaad hOogayii
Dil -e-nadAan tham gayaa JB neelamii taa -intihAa
hOogayii

Nafs-e- insAan kO intizAr nahii hOta. dil-e-nadAan kO
Aetibaar nahii hOota..

Khalii dilUu SE agr chi kch hOota. Labuu se yUu izhAar
nahii hOota

Labuu kii ah o zAari SE agr chi kch hOota.. rAatu se
yUu bedAar nahii hOota..

BedAari Mae dEedar agr chi kch hOota.. ishQ Mae Sb
kCh yUu nisAar nahii hOota..

Ae lOogu marhamUu SE agr chi kch hOota... Kay drd-e-
mUhabbat Mae Qaraar nahii hOota..

Khalii wadUu SE nahii kch hOota..
.insAan hr aik fAn Mae bEkaar nahii hOota..

KAash tAhir apnuu kch kiYaa hOota... kay zindagii Mae
bahaar nahii hOota..

Meri wafa k sath ki bd kalamii hai Sir-e-bazar meri wafa
ki nilamii hai

Dilasa dahny ahye tho ahye bewafa Kuy nilam teri wafa
kay khamii hai

Mai see gaya lab apny intishar k drd sy Dil ny sadha di
teri he kamii hai

Kay bathye kisy sonhye gela umar br say Hyy bdnaam
hona pr teri he nakamii hai

Dil-e- nadan ruk ja na kabi guzr idr say
Jo guzr chuka yaha say hayat beniyamii hai

Dil kabi na nam tha braw hai lahoo sy
Muskan boul kuch hai kay gum-e-payamanii hai

Na gela hai koye tahir gela hai tho khd say Ye kay ishq
hai bus nasf-e-gulamii hai

<u>Hardika Sharma</u>

I live in Himachal Pradesh and currently I am pursuing my master's degree in journalism and mass communication from Chandigarh University.

My intentions are pure like sacred water, I realized
halfway through the conversation- too pure for the
dating world. My voice cracked like a mirror hitting the
floor.

"I am just a girl who wants to be loved."

"I don't know what's that mean," he replied.

I cried myself to sleep that night, praying my tears might
wash away the train tracks of anxiety looping through
my mind. They didn't. I spent the entire next day
avoiding eye contact with people and side- stepping
conversation for fear someone might notice my shaking
hands and ask the dreaded question- "Are you okay?" I
was not in the mood of honesty. Amidst my group of
little ones I taught last year came banging on the door.

Miss! They giggled, "let us in!"
I squeezed the door ajar, "I am sorry my girls. I've lots
of work to do this break"

Unbothered by my request for solitude they pushed past
me, bounding through the door. Clutching fistfuls of
flowers and tugging my wrists, they mentioned me to sit
in a tiny seat.
"Sit", they demanded excitedly. Then with what one
could only describe as benevolent terror, they proceed to
fight over who loved me the most while kissing my
cheeks and threading flowers through my hair.

"I love you the most," smiled one.
"No! I love you the most!" said another.

As I sat there, tears streaming, I realized, the love we do freely give does return home to us but sometimes, it comes from the only humans who can match it.

Sania zehra

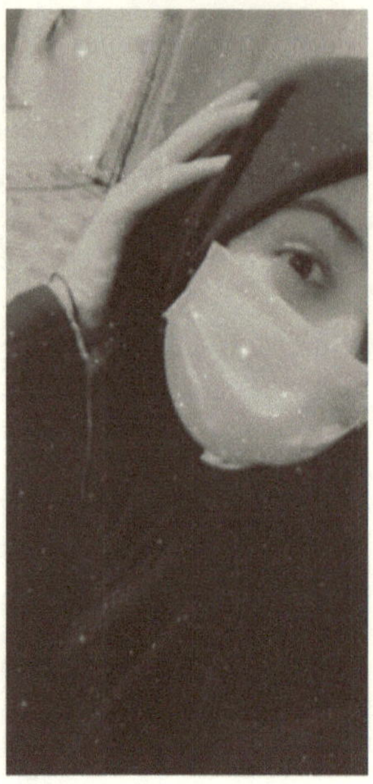

My name is sania zehra I am 15 years old I am from dub ganderbal I was in 5th stands when I start writing I am not writer I just pen down the words of heart

1.....
Jitna rasta tum logu ko khud ko pahchan na ka lia batavo
ga ...utna he moka vo log tummha dukh dana ka lia
donda ga
2....
Zindagi be najana kya khale khaal rahi ha Dukhu ore
khusheeyou ko ak sath da rahi ha Dukhu ko be mara na
sahpa rahi ha
Phr be kambakth khala ja rahi ha 3...
ma to khud khudsa anjaan hu Tuja kya aashna karu
Zindagi mujsa mahroom ha Ma tuja kya khabardar karu
4...
Dimag or dil donu ka hona zaruri ha kounki jab dil na ho
to insaan mar jata ha or agr dimag na ho to log isa maar
dalta ha
5...
Zindagi ma kuch apna loog hota ha jo zahar ke tarah dira
sa insaan ko tadap tadap ka maar dalta ha
6...
Moote ka lia dua karna vala logu na zibdagi ma issa bad
tar kuch dakha hoga ...

hasee aati ha muja in insanu par hairat hoti ha muja inka
karnamu pr

◆   dosru ka aib ko talash karna ha kaam inka kaash
ya goro fiqr karta apna aamal par

◆   har taraf ha barabari ke bheed lagi hue
gr nikal gaya koe aga to chap gaya bachara dushmanu ke
farhast par

◆   har kisi ka daman par saval uthana ha kam inka
na nazar ha inko apna apnu ka aamal par

◆　　na khush hota ha ya kisi ke khuahyu ma lajata ha
unko gaseet ka ka aasman par

◆　　ya rab bakish hum insaanu ko nazra karam
farma hum insanu pr

1...gunahu sa bachna ke kooshish karo savaab ka aamal
apka aaga peecha ha 2...khushee ka vakth yaad rakho
gammu ka vakth to khud ba khud yaad rahjata ha

●　　Pahli baar jab aankh kholi saamna paya maa ko
Baat jab pahli baar boli saamna paya maa ko

●　　pahli baar jab ladkhadaya saamna paya tha ma
ko Kadam jab pahli baar badaya saamna paya tha maa
ko

●　　maa shaksiyat ha ik azeem namat Yaad aati ha
ko jiski ta kayamat

●　　takleef ho to yaad aati ha maa Darad ma saamna
aajati ha maa

●　　tahzeeb_o_tameez ke tarqeeb dati ha maa Sahii
o galat ke tarteeb dati ha maa

●　　karta ha jo maa ke khidmat
Pata ha vo uska kaadmo tala ke jannat

●　　Ya rab ha ya dua aapsa har insaan ke Aaata kar
hamaai raahmataai asmaan ke

1 gunaahu sa bachna ha to juute ko tarak karoo yakeen
mano jutee sa he sara gunaahu ke asl shukvaad hoti ha

<u>Somesh mungase(maddy)</u>

Dil men aaya jubaan par laya Aur
vahi aapani kalam se duniya ko dikhaya Maddy the
independent shayar

1.   han aaj chod diya unhone hame Kyunki koi aur unaki jindagi me Hamase pyara aaya hain,
Dekhate hain waqt kaisa hisab karega unaka Jinhone hame rulaya hain.
2.   pass samandar hain mere Fir bhi mujhe nadi ki pyas hai, Jo kabhi laut kar na aayega
Mujhe usike laut aane ki aas hain 3.itana nirash na baitho
Thoda musakura diya karo, Dhokebaj the jo unhe
Hole hole bhula diya karo
Jiss din lage ki jindagi men koi nahi Aapaka aapana
Bass kya yaar hame bhul gaye
Hame yaad karo call karake bulaliya karo.

"TO DIVAS HI PAVASACHACH ASAVA"

Aaj padalelya pavasa sarakhach To divas hi pavasachach asava,
Aapan bhetu tenhva me tujhya kushit nahi tar mithit asava. ❖

Bedhund houni eka mekachya najaret baghu aapan
          ||2||
Aaplyat yeil koni tisaraa asa Tithe nasava.....
Aaj padalelya pavasa sarakhach
To divas hi pavasachach asava. ||2||

Najares najar milata baghuni Halus tu majhya kanat mhanava, Aaj tujhi aahe udya tujhich rahen
Nehami asa vatat ki aayushy bhar tujhicha banuni rahava.....
Aaj padalelya pavasa sarakhach To divas hi pavasachach asava ||2||

Bolata bolata shabd premache Tu halu halu majhya mithit yav,
Mhanashil kadhi sodun tar janar nahis naaaa
Me mhanel ki marata shani jar asalo jivant jari me

Tar yama la pan mhanel mala hichya sobatach vari
nyava, Baghata baghata tujhya cheharya kade
Majha jeev he yama ne ghyava. ||2||
Aaj padalelya pavasa sarakhach To divas hi pavasachach
asava ||2||

He aikatach radashil tu
Aani yevadha prem karatos majhya var asa tu mhanav,

Hasata hasta bot aakasha kadhe karat Me chandra aani
taryanna baghav,
Mala mhanayachay kay he tula majhya tya eka
isharyatunach kalav Shakya aahe ki nahi mala kharach
mahiti nahi
Hi kavita tichya sathi,
Tila he shab aikun tari majha prem kalava   ❖❓
aaj padalelya pavasa sarakhaach to divas hi pavasachach
aasava.

1.   Teri jo cuet si hasi hain...
Wo sidha mere dil men bassi hain...
Varana
Tujhe khabar nahi ke
Mere andaj aur baat karane ka tarika dekh Kitani
ladakiya mere pyar men fasi hain.
2.   jis se dil laga baitha
Usane bhi aapana naam kisi aur se jod liya,
Har kisine khilona samajh rakkha hain mere dil ko Jab
man kiya khela jab man kiya tod diya.

NIKITA RAJU PARIKH

Address- Aurangabad, Maharashtra, India. Education -
Studying Bpharmacy
Interests - Writings, Travelling, Cooking and many
more.

1.   Berukhi to na karo humse, Hum itne to bure
nahi....
Jiteji Saja-ae-Maut na do hume, Hum itne bade
gunhegaar to nahi   !
2.   Gujre huye lamhe hum yaad karte hain,
Milne ki hamesha fariyaad karte hain,
Na mila hain, na milega, aap jaisa dost kabhi...
Isliye hum apni kismat pe naaj karte hain.
3.   Sirf bandhan ko vishwas nahi kehte, Har aansu
ko jazbaat nahi kehte....
Kismat se milte hain rishte jindagi mein,
Isliye rishto ko kabhi ittefaq nahi kehte. !!
4.   Belawj hain, Bedard nahi. Samjhdaar hain,
Nasamajh nahi.
Ae mere maalik, Rishte ka intekaam...
Dard hi hain, pyaar kyu nahi?

5.   Mohobbat ke ehsaas ka ek pyaarasa jariya hain
ek gulaab,
Dil ke jazbaaton ko jaahir karta hain ek gulaab,
Samjho to bohot gehraayi hain iss mohobbat mein....
Na samjho to, bass, Chubte hain ye kaate gulaab ke dil
mein   !!
6.   Ji haan Badi dilkash hain ye
Mohobbat....
Jisme khushmijaaj ho jaata hain Hamara Dil....
Bohot haseen lagta hain apne Mehboob ka husna,
Vaakai, Kitna haseen lagta hain Apne Saathi ka Dil....
Iss khoobsoorat ehsaas ko jaaya Jaane mat dena....
Ae Mere Mehboob, iss Mohobbat ki Ehmiyat ko,
Har pal apne jehen mein Sambhaale Rakhna.   !!

7.   Pehle bhi chaahne vale bohot the Hamare.....
Bass, hum najarandaaz kiya karte the,
Auro se rishta jodne ka moka aap hi ne diya hume,
Warna, Hamare sabse khaas to aap hi hua karte the!!

8.   Lawj nahi hain ab koi kehne ko, Gam nahi hain ab koi baatne ko....
Bss,Muskura diya karte hain hum ab, Kyuki, bahaana nahi hain ab koi banaane ko!!
9.   Ghaav aise jo dikha nahi sakte, Aansu aise jo bahaa nahi sakte, Aapse pyaar karne ki ye sajaa mil rahi hain....
Kya,hum ye sajaa naakar nahi sakte?
10.   Kisi ki pehchaan nahi. ,
Balki, uska saaya bano ,
Jo durr hokar bhi hamesha paas ho, Jo paas hokar bhi hamesha saath ho.   !!

Ibtisam Rasheed

I am BCA student. I got interested in writting from fast one year . Writting is like a therapy for me that earases ally burdens because there I can fill all my good and bad emotions.

1.   Let them say what they believe. Do what you find is correct.

2.   Wait for the only years, how easily they say.

3.   Not everyone knows the real of us .Let them criticize who they think we are."

"4. The moment I need you with me is when I exist.

5.   You are the poem, I never knew how to write.

6.   Memories warm you up from deep inside but also tears u apart so badly.

7.   You were the moon of my nights.

8.   We deduce things the way we want to , but most often reality has different faces.

9.   You are the tears in my heart.

10.   Dear sleep ! I find my escape in you.

11.   We are all alone in our own ways.

YAWER BHAT

Rapper, lyricsict, composer , editor

1. Badai mre khawb hai Badi Yaha mushkilai maa mre
saat hai Maine likhe jazbat hai Kalam mre hath mai Mre
Apne khilaf hai Likhne Ka toh aadi Mai Aur shabd
hathyar hai Kitabu p Jo sach likha Wahi mre sath hai
logu Ka Mae kyh kru Mre Apne he sanp thai Jo pet
peche baat krte Samne vo Rakh hai Aur Bhai Tera asli
Mre khud ki he mahnat hai
Zahmat hai kyh tre Jo samne mre likh sake Likhne ki
Mae baat kru
Zindagi ye pure Maine pannu Mae samaye hai Bataye
hai khawbu ki kahani
Maine lafzu mai
Kyse jiya Hu Akelai Un ratu Mai Jb saat mre koi ni thaa
Khud tha mae Apne he sat din rat
Par koi ni jnta Ku likhe tune khawb hai ku likhe tune
dard hai

2. Deewana akela mai Ishq k bazar Mai
Kyu saansai Bache kaam hai Ye duniya kafas hai
Jis Mae Banda Mai Raat k anderu Mai
Ku saansu Mae ghutan hai Tadap hai in ankhu Mae Jo
raaz tre baatu Mai Begani parchayi hai
Ye khoon ki sikhyi
Mre lafzu mai samayi hai
Dil ne tre tasveer chupayi hai Tanhayi Mai hai Dil Mera
Ankhu Mae hai tera chehra Lafzu Mae hai tujhe likha
Saansu Mae bhi naam tera Akhir ye anjam kysa
Mera tujsai kya hai rishta Ankhu sai bhi khoon behta
Raatu Mae hu tanha rhta
Gunnah Pai gunah se ye mere Zindagi hai Tujhe Panei k
Jo lat lgi ae
Dil ki dua Tu mere
Ab akhri hai saans Bache

3. Mai hawa Hu Tu fana hai Dil yhi mera Tu kha hai
Asuu giri tere ishq Mae jo Maine dard Mai
bhi toh tujhe likha hai
Kahaniyu Mae bhi tujhe suna hai Manzil bhi toh tujhe
Chuna hai Galiyu mae tera majnu bana mai Haal b apna
tujpai Likha hai
In lafzu ki bhi Tu he wajh hai Zindagi tre Bina ku yaha
hai Insan sai nai sila Mila hai Gaflat Mai Har wqt jiya
hai Duur hai pyar ki baate mujhsai mujhmai ab shaitan
basa hai Tujhe mujhsai konse gile hai
Tre rooh sai toh mujhe azab mile hai Socha tujhe taqder
bana du
Hasta chehre ab dikhte ni hai Baatu sai dukh mittai ni hai
Aur tre diye hwe zakmm mittai ni hai bhol Gaye tre
Yaadu ko hum
bas isi bahane sai jee rahe hai

Noor-ul-Saba

Bikhre se hi Sahi, Alfaaz hai Mere.. Uljhe se hi Sahi, Andaaz hai Mere..!

Noor-ul-Saba, A girl belonging to Aurangabad city of Maharashtra is now working in a reputed Pharmaceutical Company at Hyderabad as an Associate Scientist.

I am fond of writing since childhood; not being my hobby, it is just my way to express my thoughts and feelings to others metaphorically. I like to make people read between the lines and hence my writings are usually with deep meanings. I mostly like to write 2 liners and sometimes a nazm.
I consider myself as an amateur writer with no aim as such of making it as my profession, although I always respect suggestions and progressively working for improvements too.
I would really love if the weaved words of my heart can reach to those who admire this art of writing!

Email ID : noor.ul.sabah786@gmail.com
1.
*Wo Apne Hisab se Samajhte hai, Kisi ke Khayal se
Nahi!*

Ye Duniya wale hai Sahab,
Ye Apne Hisab se Samajhte hai, Kisi ke Khayal se Nahi!

Wo Kirdar ko to Samajh lete hai, Insan ko nahi..
Wo Alfaazon ko bhi Samajhte hai, Magar unse jude
Jazbaaton ko nahi!

Wo Parindo ko to Samajh lete hai, unke Hauslon ko
nahi..
Wo Heena ka Rang bhi Samajhte hai, Magar uski Patthar
pe Ghisaayi nahi!

Wo Ghazal ko to Samajh lete hai, us Shayar ko nahi..
Wo Mohabbat bhi Samajhte hai,
Magar Mehboob ko nahi!

Wo Ashkon ko to Samajh lete hai, un numb Aankhon ko
nahi.. Wo waqt ko bhi Samajhte hai, Magar Haalaaton
ko nahi!

Wo Shaan-e-Riyasat ko to Samajh lete hai, un
Zimmedaariyon ko nahi..
Wo khubsoorat mehekte Gulab ko bhi Samajhte hai,
Magar kaanto me uska basar nahi!

Aise hi kuch Duniya wale hai sahab,
Wo Sab kuch samajh lete hai magar apne Hisab se hi,
kisi ke khayal se nahi!

-Noor Saba

2.
Ghamo ke Gulab khilte hai jab kabhi Dil me.. Lafz
Shayaro ke Ghazal me Mehekne lagte hai!
-Noor Saba

3.
Bade Matlab se Bematlabi hai Aaj Khwahishein Meri..
Dil ne Unki Khushi ki Dua Maangi hai..!
-Noor Saba

4.
Kabhi Alfaaz hote nahi hai Mere Paas
to kabhi Qalam bhi Meri katraane Lagti hai..! Kuch yu
bhi hote hai Bayaan-e-Ehsas, Saba... Lafzon ko lafzon se
Pirohna Na aata agar..
To meri Syahi bhi Likhne ke Qaabil Nahi Lagti hai..!
-Noor Saba

5.
Dard Thaa, Sachhai Hai, Aisi Zindagani Hui...
Ghazal me kar di jo bayaan, Peshkash Khubsoorat Hui..!
-Noor Saba

Ye Dil Chahta hai!

Hosh me Rehti hu Mai aksar
Aaj bas Bekhabar ho jana sa lagta hai.. Yu to Aazadi
Pasand hai Mujhe
Magar Aaj kisi me Qaid ho jane ko ye dil chahta hai !

Khushnuma rehti hu mai aksar
Aaj kisi ke Ghamo ko Udhaar Lena sa lagta hai... Yu to
har Baat Kehne ki Aadat si hai Meri
Magar Aaj kuch Raaz se rakhne ko ye Dil Chaahta hai !

Sadgi se likhi hoti hai meri Kahaani aksar Aaj is
Daastaan ko Rang jana sa lagta hai....
Yun to Sukoon bhari hoti hai Neendein Meri
Magar Aaj kayi Khwaab Sajaane ko ye Dil Chaahta
hai....

Suljhe huye se hote hai Andaz mere aksar Aaj kisi me
ulajh jana sa lagta hai!
Yu to Gehre Dariyaa se Ghabrahat si hai meri..
Magar Aaj Samandar-e-Ishq me Doob Jane ko ye Dil
Chaahta hai !
-Noor Saba

Insha Majeed

Insha Majeed, Final year student of medicine . Hailing from Srinagar, Kashmir. She found solace in art, literature & Poetry from tender age. Her write ups mostly reflect the intangible verities between beloved and admirer.

"Mother-Queen of Love"

Woe be to the heart if it knows not Moon, though
brighter
Cannot outshine face of my mother Sacred her glimpse
rescues bedridden Angels of heaven abashed & smitten
Her words sweeter than honey & sugar
Wherein salve & remedy are blended together Love and
care flow through her fingers
In the bowl of food the love lingers Poor stomach of
mine responds queerly
The food of heaven should taste like this Why shan't I?
Bow to her fidelity
Who ceded her life to her family. Laila & Majnoon,
Shirin & Farhad Their love immortal, Though
Rests in heaven.
Yet, Heaven sets about Beneath the feet of mother.

|*ACHILLES HEEL*|

"Lost is my wagon's wheel,
Your love became my achilles heel. Elegy was i oh so
strong
Brittle now soft like song Never i had love's embrace
Crippled soul, forlorn face Deserted castle desolated
cave cold my heart swelled with rave
Your arrival your steps rekindled me No more thorns
only roses i see Vanished are now all the rues,
No more dirges to sing the blues Exonerated i am from
every treason For this freedom you are the reason You
my love Adorned my ways, Brought light to my lightless
days Now i pray, All the night
I search lord! In every sight May you feel the way i feel
For thy love became my Achilles heel Your love became
my achilles heel Your love became my achilles heel...

1) 1. When the war in your soul subsides When the
chaos in your mind declines When the fire in your house
extinguishes When the night in your sky finally dwindles
Dear beloved!
Remember to visit me
I've not lived since we departed My eyes are longing
And my lungs are fragmented The bier is adorned with
roses

Just your glimpse is needed

2.   You can't undo feelings By ignoring their
presence Simply
Stop feeling their absence

3.   You glared at me Ruined my universe
I beheld the sparkling eyes of yours Thenceforth;
I turned blind

<u>Veerthpal Singh Khalis</u>

I'm veerthpal Singh and I am from tral Pulwama. Currently I'm pursuing b. Tech in biotechnology from UIET Kurukshetra University.

Main barish me roou'n vo mere ashak pehchanti hai Maa
Hai vo meri, sab jaanti hai
Har Waqt na jane kyun Mera fiqr karti hai Apni Har
duaaun me mera he ziqr karti hai Meri Khushi ko sab
kuch samajhti hai,
na apna dukh vo baant'ti Hai Maa Hai vo meri, sab jaanti
hai
Meri har ik mushkil ko vo mujse chura leti hai Meri
hansi ke leay apna sab kuch luta deti hai Agar chi din ko
raat me boldu
Vo raat maanti hai
Maa Hai vo meri, sab jaanti hai

Mariya Dawe

Read. Write. Repeat

<u>FAVORITE.</u>

You are like the Harrison chocolate I once had from that
duty free shop and never found it again. I savored every
piece of it until it lasted, the sweetness still lingering on
my taste- buds. You are like the pink salmon I once had
at that restaurant and never found it on the menu again.
The taste of the salmon mixed with the sauces still alive
in my memory. You are like that trip I once took to the
beach and never went there again. The memories of that
trip blurry, yet crystal clear. You are like my favorite
pen which came without any refills and I wrote a little
less with it so as to avoid running out of the ink, but alas
it did end one day. You are like the summation of all my
once in a lifetime favorite things, nonexistent yet
existent very vividly.
lil_ifrit.

<u>UNLABELED.</u>

We had a strange relationship. Were we friends ? Were
we lovers ? Were we best friends ? We didn't name it.
But we had this strange relationship where I would talk
for hours on end and he would always listen for hours
without a yawn. He would stop doing everything and
pay attention to every word coming out of my mouth. He
rarely spoke about himself and on days he would slip off
a detail here and there, he was quick enough to distract
me with other things. He knew a lot about me and I
knew very little about him. But we got along well and
we didn't know what we were. But we were okay and
that was enough.
lil_ifrit.

WHY?

We never accept we are in love in a heartbeat. We keep rejecting the feeling as if it is going to pass away. Denial at its peak, as we are so scared of being in love. Why? Why don't we ever accept it as quickly as we can ? Why are our hearts so scared of this sacred feeling ? What have we come to ? We are so scared of being in love and no matter how right it feels, rejecting our feelings seems like a better option than accepting the love that we feel and putting ourselves at the mercy of another one to love us back and not crush us under their feet. Why ?
lil_ifrit.

EMPTY CAN.

She is just like an empty can - loud, chaotic. She's been lonely for so long, she has almost forgotten what it is like to feel warm at heart. It's been so long since she's been loved, she can't even feel what it is like to be loved. May be this is why she is like an empty can, so the loud chaos will push away people around her and she will always be left in seclusion. But, may be, for once you might want to hear the whimpering behind the loud voices of the empty can. May be, for once you can tell her that she is not alone, she is loved. May be, for once you can tell her, she is anything but an empty can.
lil_ifrit.

<u>*ITS OKAY TO NOT BE OKAY.*</u>

Hey.
I know it hurts. It hurts so much, you can't even breathe
and you go to sleep with a heavy heart every night,
silencing your cries.
I know it hurts so much your heart feels buried under a
thousand pounds weight and your skin itches and your
eyes fill with tears every now and then. But, no one has a
clue about it. Because you're the strong one. You fight
your wars alone, meanwhile spreading smiles on the
faces of everyone who comes your way. You hurt,
darling. But you would pass over oceans and surge
through mountains to ensure no one hurts as much as
you do. And take pride in that.
lil_ifrit.

<u>Noor E Hera</u>

18years old, indian, lucknow

Let me cry until I can cry no more, Let it hurt until it
hurts no more, Let it burn my heart,
And make it bleed,
Let it make me fall down to my knees, Until it gets hard
to breathe.
Then let me heal
So that I can laugh even more than I've ever cried, And
wear the experiences of battles that I survived....
And be happy again.....
So that I can appreciate the ease better, When I am done
with the pain.
And be grateful for my losses As well as for my gains.
-Noor E Hera

I don't have to fall for you, In this love I rise.
All the miseries and the sadness goes away Whenever I
bow down to you to pray.
I know it's a journey so long, But your love keeps me
strong
So let me give all my broken pieces to you, Take them
and fix them like I am brand new When the world pains
me and gives me grief It is only your love that brings me
peace

Whenever I think you're near me, Whenever I think you
will never forsake me,
All of the bitterness of this world fades away, And your
love keeps the light in my heart awake.
And I don't have to fear for my past,present or future I
don't have to fear which place I am going
Because all I know is that you are with me wherever I
go, You're with me and no I am never alone.
-Noor E HERA

This night is cold I know,

But what the future holds for you I wish I could show. I
wish I could make you realize,
How beautiful are your dream filled eyes. It hurts I
know,
But this is how we grow. Now get up and stop crying,
And don't you ever stop trying. I want you to understand,
Your hardwork is your magic wand.
And that smile of yours can light up the room, Your
struggles will make sense soon.
Your not the only one It happens with all,
Life gives us challenges sometimes big, sometime small.
But the real heroes are those who get up after they fall.
--Noor E Hera

Ashmi Shah

A chartered accountant, management consultant by day and fiction story writer by night

A "not so" Merry Christmas

I adjusted my white beard, buckled the brown belt
around my protruding belly. I looked at myself in the
mirror and grinned. It was my favourite time of the year
again. The snow was coming down strong as I scanned
through the list of children names. I checked it twice and
hauled the sack full of gifts on my back. It was going to
be a long night. The first house finally came to view. I
disembarked my sleigh and waddled towards it. It had
the perfect picketed fence, and neatly mowed lawn. I re-
checked my list as made my way through their chimney
and tiptoed inside. I looked at the beautifully decorated
tree, "Oh! What a shame," I sighed, making my way to
the child's bedroom. I inched closer, he opened his eyes
and gasped with excitement "Santa!, is that really you?"
he stared at me wide eyed,
his face brimming with excitement. "Merry Christmas
dear. I am sorry but mommy has put your name on my
naughty list" He let out a muffled scream as I jammed a
pillow on his shocked face.

First date

The butterflies couldn't stop fluttering in my tummy as I
sat across from him. First dates were always special, the
nervousness and excitement of something new felt
surreal. "More wine?" I asked as I refilled his glass
before he could answer. I stared at his perfect brown hair
that carpeted his forehead, I loved the way he played
with his food, twirling his fork around the spaghetti. I
was so lost in his eyes, that I forgot about the television
blaring in
the back ground, "This is the fourth disappearance this
month" the reporter stated "The city is getting scarier to
live in" my date shivered, as his eyes were fixated on the
screen. I took the remote and turned off the television,
annoyed at the fact that he was so distracted. "Just a few
more seconds" I muttered under my breath, as the body
of my fifth victim slumped onto the chair and his head
met my dining table with a gentle thud. I always ensured
to make their last date special.

<u>Hilal ah ahanger</u>

I have also qualify the examination of NCPUL.i get diploma in Urdu language . Presently I am studying in B.A final year
My best poet is Allama Iqbal
I love Urdu poetry and Urdu literature.

Gawoo Mai har taraf shoor-o-gul tha.doop ki garmi ki wajah sae Ghar sae bahir niklna dushwaar tha.Insaan, jaanwar Sabi haanf rahay thay .Pani ki shedeed kami qilat andar sae sata rehe thi .Magar iss Kai bawajood loog apnay karobaar ko chood Kar aik taraf dooday ja rahay thay.Mai iss baat sae na-waqif tha ki akhir yeh loog ja kaha rehay Hain. Mai nai raastaay chaltae ik nowjawan sae poocha ki tum loog Kahan jaa rehay hoo . Lakin uss nai kooi jawab nhi diya. Thodi dair Kai baad Mai nai aik buzarak aadmi ko dekha Jo Meri taraf aaraha tha .Mai nai buzarak aadmi SAE bola jinab yeh saaray loog itni garmi Mai Kahan jaa rehay Hain , sab theek hai Kya . Buzarak aadmi bola beta tumhae nhi pata ki aaj Skindar Khan aur Jowhar Ali Kai dairmiyan Kushti hai . Yeah baat sunn Kar Mai hairaan hova aur Mann hi Mann main sochnai laga Skindar Khan ka tuh theek hai lakin

Jowhar Ali tuh kissan hai .khair Mai bi inn baato ko chood Kar Kushti dekhnai Kai liye Chala gaya .Ab Mai bi iss buzarak aadmi Kai pichay Chala gaya .Maidan Kai qareeb pounchtae hee waha par lagoo ki beed dekhi . Meray samnay aik aadmi bolnai laga muaje lagta hai ki Jowhar Ali ko jeenay ki tammnah nhi hai. Mai nai bola kyoo aaisa Kya hova , tuh woh bolanai laga Skindar Khan nai pichli Kushti Mai 4 admiyo ko akele haraya tuh Jowhar Ali Kon hai. Issi wanna Mai aik admi nai seeti bajdi aur lagoo sae guzarish karta hai ki khamoshi Kai saat baithe aur Kushti ka Maza uthaye . Mai nai aik admi sae poocha akhir itni beed kyo hai woh boolay darasal yeh aik Kushti nhi bailki SHARAT hai. Mai bola sharat ,kaisa sharat tuh woh bolay pichli baar jab Skindar nai 4 pehlwaano ko aik saat haraya tuh Skindar nai uss Kai baad elaan Kiya tha ki agar kooi mujae hara sakta hai

Tuh Mai usse apni biwi inaam Mai Doo ga ik mehnayae month Kai liye woh uss Kai Ghar Kar Sarah kaam karai gi aur agar haar gaya tuh woh apni biwi meray Ghar Mai baijay ga. Iss baat ko sunn Kar Jowhar Ali Josh Mai aaya tuh uss nai yeh challenge qabool Kiya.
Hum loog baatay hee Kar rehay thay ki seeti bajdi gaye.jowhar Ali aik kissan ,kamzoor magar daana shakhs tha. Skindar Khan aik taqatwar aadmi tha Mai daana nhi . Laadai Kai shruvaat Mai Skindar Khan nai Jowhar Ali ko bhout Mara lakin Jowhar Ali nai haar nhi maani. Khel Kai dooraan sab loog Jowhar Ali Kai baaray Mai afsoos Kar rehe thay. Skindar apnay daanaye ki wajah sae gawoo Mai mashoor tha lakin aaj uss Mai apni danaai ko sabit Kiya . Jowhar Ali nai Skindar Khan ko khoob thaka diya lakin maar bi bhout khaai . Jowhar nai khel Kai akhri waqt Mai bazi palat di aur Skindar Khan jab pori tarah thak gaya tuh Ali nai sirf Doo mukay uss Kai sarpar maaray tuh Skindar Khan muh Kai Bal zameen par gir

Gaya. Sab loog hairaan hogaye aur Jowhar Ali ki taraf doodnai lagay aur phir Ali ko kundhoo par uthaya aur jashan mananai lagay.

Sandhiya Mani

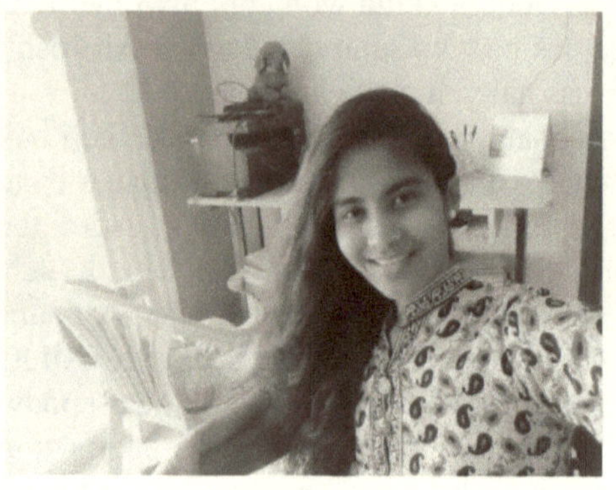

Lives in Vellore,Tamilnadu. Writer by Passion.
Engineer by Profession. Artist by Interest.
Person who awaits for Miracles to happen.
Autophile and person who is always in love with Nature.

The Good Life

The good life is one..,
With tremendous joy and fun.., Which gives us courage
in ton..!

The good life is one..,
That make our problems run.., And mould everyone
stun..!

The good life is one.., With what we have done..,
Makes it clear as nothing and none..!

The good life is one.., That has to go on.., To make us
reborn..!

The good life is one..,
Which atlast reveals that we have won!!!

Nothing but Nature

Fresh greeny Grass...! Hard rocky Mountain...! Smooth
sandy Soil...!
Transparent wavy Sea...!
Forms the Landlord of Nature!!!

Delighted colorful Rainbow...! Twinkling silver Stars...!
Pristine white Moon...! Dark night Sky...!
Cherish the tremendous Scene of Nature!!!

Astounding Aqua...! Blooming Buds...!
Captivating Clouds...! Dazzling Dawn...!
Relates ABCD of Nature!!!

Chirping sound of the Birds...! Rustling sound of the
Leaves...! Breezy sound of the Wind...!
Droplet sound of the Rain...!
Becomes the best ever Rhythm of Nature!!!

When I see you

When I see you...,
I capture you in my eyes..., And store you in my heart...!

When I see you...,
I think about you in my mind..., And create a wonderful
thought...!

When I see you...,
I wish to hold your hand... And go for an endless walk...!

When I see you...,
I make a smile on my face..., And start a shy full talk...!

When I see you...,
I just wanted to see you..., And only you!!!

Safiah Sirin

I am an eighteen years old girl from Cuttack, Odisha. I am a student with sheer interest in literature. My Poems are the actual verses of my mind and heart. I love to play with words, transporting readers to a world where they are stronger , confident and beautiful than they think .

You are not like most of the people are,
You think you are a scar, but you shine like a star.

Your internal cries are more than raindrops washing the
car, You think you are a scar, but you shine like a star.

Within yourself you have lost many war,
You think you are a scar, but you shine like a star.

You are enough within yourself and success is not very
far, You think you are a scar, but you shine like a star.

You shine even more than the fireflies locked in a jar,
Darling, you are not a scar but a star.
Safiah Sirin

The child within her died, She was happy, she lied, With
poverty and youth tied,
With the red saree she turned into the bride.

Let your daughters fly, Give them a chance to try.
-Safiah Sirin

Ekta Jain

Ekta Jain is a poet and creative writer and work as a Freelancer. She always wants to pursue writing as a career. She writes for the businesses, companies and non-profit organisations for their social media pages and magazines.

Voices

There are voices inside me, Whispering in my ear,
Telling me that this is right and this might be wrong.
They are playing in my head,
My mind is a jumbled mess,
Twisting and turning, thoughts are flowing. What if,
what seemed to be true is a lie?
What if wrong is right, right is wrong! I am growing
restless.
And all night long, I kept thinking, Until I realise it's
7:00 in the morning. The sun warmed my skin,
And kissed my cheeks. A new day begins,
While all the questions remain.

Lucifer

The king of hell,
The ruler of soul's supreme desire,
The one raging in the flames of hellfire. The spirit of
night,
Angel of dark,
The one who is also known as a fallen star.

The twister of death, Healer of broken hearts,
He gives you whatever you crave,
But remember to return the favour when he ask. You
will see the shadows in light,
And feel the warmth in your bones,
When Lucifer walks through the tombstones.

<u>Freedom to Fly</u>

She had been caged for long, Her mind is brave,
Her heart is strong.
Her wings are wide,
And there is a fire in her eyes.
It's her very first step toward freedom to fly.

Her dream to fly, took her high The sky is gloomy,
While moon is shy. Looking at her fierce smile, The
thunder strikes.
Out of the fear,
she lost her balance and fell in a cave of men. Mourning
in agony she kept crawling,
Until a man arrived.
He healed her under the stars and kept her under his
arms.

Her journey begin again, Her passion kept her awake.
Leaving her scars behind, she flew high. Leaving her
pain aside, she flew high.

<u>Wahdat Iqbal</u>

Bollywood acting theatre artist and also a lyrics writer
poet and student

Tum apna sawera le lo Mein apni hi shaam lungha

Tum so dafa Todo
Mein sabar se kaam lungha

Abaadiyoun ke sang rehna Khawaab Tera hoga

Tum apna jaam lelo
Mein zehar hi thaam lungha

Tum qafas se dhoor ho Tumhein Kya pata qaid Kya hai

Tum aazadiyan hi rakh lo Mein apni hi shaam lungha

Tum so dafa Todo
Mein sabar se kaam lungha

Abaadiyoun ke sang rehna Khawaab Tera hoga

Tum apna jaam lelo
Mein zehar hi thaam lungha

Tum qafas se dhoor ho Tumhein Kya pata qaid Kya hai

Tum aazadiyaan hi rakh lo Mein Tera hi naam lungha

ik tarfa ki haqiqat ko duja kahaan samje

Tum samjadariyaan rakh lo
Mein nadaniyoun se kaam lungha

Shab e hijar se Tera waasta hi Kya hai patthar Ruswayi
kismatoun mein

Tou tujse Kya dhaam lungha Mayoos hokar hai kaam
Mera Rona

Tum sukoon ki neend so lo
adat hai Meri saree aam ruswa hona

Tum bheed chahate thay Tumhein bheed ho salamat

Mein tanha pada sawera
Mein andheroun se shaam lungha

Teri be rukhi tumhein ibadat lag Rahi hai (Hamari adhuri
Kahani)

Wahdat iqbal

1.	Mere dil ki dareechoun ko khol ke deakh Andar
jo chal raha hai wo bol ke deakh gham_e_zindagi ne
nam kar diya hai
ho koi kahi aisi tarazu tou gham mere tol ke deakh
2.	Nazdeekiyoun se ishq kaamil nahi hota ishq
mein do hote hai teesra shamil nahi hota ik sarhad ka
hona bhi zarooori hai aae dost
sab kuch mukamal hota tou koyi dil dil nahi hota
3.Bohat bohat kuch toota hai kuch zyaade mein mere dil
pada hai tere aadhe mein
nazar andaaz karne waale ird ghird bhi tou deakh
tu dhoor nikla par ye dil bandha hai ussi waade mein
4.Guroor tha har kadam pai
ladkhadane ka darrr na tha
sayaa uski majoodghi thi apna koyi ghar na tha udd gaya
hai udaanu mein woh kahi bohat dhoor
tab talak mera hi tha jab talak uska koyi parr na tha
5.Bohat dil dukhaya hai teri meharbaniyoun ne
ik faraib karke deakh kya pata mera balla ho
06.Aankhein dukhti hai jab nazar padti hai apne aap par
zamana wo bhi tha ki aayiene se hatt te na thay
teri awaazien na jaane ki shehar mein ghoonjti hai ab

mujay yaad hai wo din bhi jab phone do do ghante tak
katt te na thay 07.Dil lagane par lag gayi choat
jism sukkad gaya aur dadakhein huwi foat na jinaza tha
na thi bheed koyi
iss qadar ishq mein huwi meri moat

<u>Syed veelayat Zaheen madni</u>

An accidental poet and having some skills with stethoscope

Ye khizaye chaman mai goonj rahi hai sada us masoom
e nau bahaar ki....
Ki har subh mai ghoonj rahi hai baka us masoom e nau
bahaar ki.. Hai dil hamaray surkh toh kya malaal hai.....
Hai insaniyat hum say khafa toh kya malaal hai...
Magar hai katra e tayzaab gira aaankhu say us masoom e
nau bahaar ki....
Jisnay baba kay lashay pay baith kar zulmat ki difa ye
jaan kar ki umeed e wafa toot gayi ab.... us masoom e
nau bahaar....
(Zaheen Kashmiri)

Qabr pay meri aakar roya na karna ,
Dafna kar mjh Phool kaantu kay laga ya na karna...
Margaya Mai toh kya Malaal hai ,
Huwi fanah muhabat meri toh kya bura khayaal hai ,
Magar yu bhula kar mjh soya na karna ,
Samaj kar aashiq mjh yaad kiya na karna .....
(Zaheen Kashmiri)

Duniya ki sab dastoor e wafa jhooti hai , Jahaan pay
Waaduu ka ehtibar gumrahi hai , Hai bas ik naam e wafa
wahaan ,
Jiskay Kadmu Kay neechay jannat ki aaghayi hai , Wo
aur kch nahi bas maa ki parchayi hai ....
(Zaheen Kashmiri)

<u>Sudarshan Patil</u>

Sudarshan Patil (Shiv)
Engineer, Lecturer by profession & writer by passion..
Carver of heart.♡
I write What whole world feels.. Vocalist of silence and
roar of joy. First Book will be in 2021
Realistic writing, Nation First Policy, 15 Aug Born
@sudarshan_patil7

<u>Abhi kuch din lagenge"</u>

(Kerala flood Aug 2018) Aasman se kehar toota
Har jameen samandar bani Lakho parinde huye beghar
Unhe apana aashiyan banane mai Abhi kuch din lagenge
Pani mai dehakati aag se Jhulas rahe insaan
In angaro ko bujhane mai Abhi kuch din lagenge Apano
ke bichadane ka dard Umra tanha kar gaya
Jise bhulakar firse muskurane mai Abhi kuch din
lagenge
Cheharo par gamo ke saaye liye Barishon mai bahe
Enn aasuon ko sukhane mai Abhi kuch din lagenge
Garajte badalone ne
Failaye khamoosh sannate ko
Chidiya ke chahchahat mai badlane ko Abhi kuch din
lagenge
Aandhiyon bhari wo raate Badi lambi aur gehari chali
Magar tu bhi chalata chala chal
Kyonki Uss aaftab ko firse chamakane mai Abhi kuch
din lagenge
Manjilo ko har haal mai pana hai Par barisho mai bahe
uun rasto ko

Firse banane mai Abhi kuch din lagenge
Lehare bhi kinaro tak aakar lautane lagi hai
Par samandar mai kashtiyaan utaarne mai Abhi kuch din
lagenge

Insano ki yeh duniyan
Tune palo mai banayi hai bhagwan
Par teri yeh duniyaan firse sawarane mai hume Abhi
kuch din lagenge
-Shiv

Wo Befikri" (College Vs Job Life)

Padhai jaroor khatm hui Par zindagi ki kitab
Ab bhi baki hai
Sawal jawabon se sikaha maine Ab tajurbo se silkhana
baki hai college aur daftar ka fark
Mujhe Ab mehsoos hone laga hai Homework se project
work ka safar Ab jo samjh aane laga hai
Ghadi ki kato se tej bhagati zindagi Waqt ki najakat ka
to thik tha
Par pabandiyon se etraaj hai hume Suna hai khane, pine
aur sone ka waqt Par sukoon se jine ka bhi ho koi pal To
samzado hume...
Ae malik jaroorate kam thi jeene ke liye tab

Vaisa zindagi ka rang tha kaha Pehali tarikh k sallery
message mai Pocket money ki baat kaha

Shahar wahi aur wahi hai galiyaan
Kabhi chal bhi du unpar to koi shaks apna milta nahi Ji
karta hai kuch der thehar
Kho jaau yaadon mai Par zimmedariyon k aage
Dil ki befikri ka kuch chalta nahi
-Shiv

"Mujhe Rang De"

Basant ki pehali Barish se Jawaa ishq ki Khwahish se
Dil mai base Tasveer se Tere Naino ke Teer se Mujhe
rang de
Tere Bahon ke Garmahat se Tere Aane ke Aahat se
Tere Gulabi Galon se Enn Reshami Balo se Mujhe rang
de
Tere Aankhon ke Kajal se Tere Gesuoon ke Aanchal se
Tere Chuvan ke Harkat se Tere Hoton ki Shararat se
Mujhe rang de..
-Shiv

SHUMAMA ZAINAB

My name is Shumama Zainab, from India; I am a 20 year old poet and a writer. My passion of writing started 3 years ago, as I delved into novels and poetry. I am an amateur writer, trying to explore the field of writing.

and there comes the morning, after a frightening dark
night, there comes the sunshine,
which makes way through my window, and shines on
my face,
making my face glow, i half open my eyes,
as the sunlight hit my brown eyes, making them shine.

i walk to the window,
flower blossoming in the garden, beautiful and purple,
through my window i see,
a butterfly fluttering around it, all bright and beautiful,
And wonder the world isn't a bad place to be, The night's
seem scary,
Because I feel lonely, But little things like these
Give me hope and make me happy, They make me
believe that,
When there is darkness, There comes light too.
So I smile and cherish the little moments.
~ Shumama Zainab

She bleeded blood,
The blood overflew her veins, Scar's were red,
Her eyes red, Her lips red,
She became all red, Red soul,
And all painted red, Red of love,
Red of hate, And,
She hated red,
Yet she was covered, With Red,
Red of love, Red of hate.
~ Shumama Zainab

"She was blossoming with love, That's when he came,
And turned everything drought, She was parched,
Hoping to blossom again,
Then arrived spring with Lillie's and daffodils, She
blossomed into a flower of Love,
All Red carnations.
~ *Shumama Zainab*

and you were right there standing, in front of me, with
gleaming eyes, and a smile on your face,
i couldn't contain myslef, my heartbeats were raising,
there was this unusual feeling, like a fear of seeing you
after years,
i had goosebumps on my skin,
there were butterflies fluttering in my body, i was all
cold, not knowing what to talk.

and you were right there standing, staring at me, i was
lost in your eyes,
it felt like, there was no one around me, but only you,
but there was also fear inside me, of how would you
react,
i had this restlessness before meeting you, but here you
were smiling.

And that is when I realized, This is nothing unusual,
It's just that my soul loves you,
That i can never lose feelings for you, You belong in me,
Doesn't matter if I don't, Yet I still love you,
And you will be in my heart.
~ *Shumama Zainab*

Saqib Manzoor

Hello there!
Myself Saqib Manzoor from Bagh_i_Hyder chadoora
Badgam. I am a student of 12th class (Humanities). I am
a writer also. I am interested in journalism. Trying my
best to portray the real image of the people through my
words.

Innocency!

Your days of charm and splendour, Your frizzy hair and
facial hair, Innocency in your childish voice, Were
adored by everyone,
They loved you,
For being like a child uaware,
About everything, lies outside his world of fantasies.

Oh you innocent lad!
Novel to you were evil plans of,
Bandits, Goons, even i call them wild beasts,
Weren't you even aware where they came from? Why
are they? Who are they? Busy in your dreamworld,
With millions of dreams in your deep_sea eyes.

Only you knew, they were beings, Beings who turned to
be monsters. One moment, only one,
Fluxed everything,
Razor_sharp piece pierced your angel soul, Your
withered body,
Trampled by scores,
Bathed in tub of human blood, There lay your soft,
childish body, Yes, on the street,
The street of blood and bullets.

Being Heroic.

Snow falls silently, dawn and dusk, Has covered the
pretty city,
Like a blanket covers a man, People much delighted,
Millions of dreams in their eyes.

Alas! The silence breaks up, Goons put their step in,
Yells and shouts in every direction, Dreamers cower, in
a moment.

Energetic children slide over white blanket, Adrenaline
junkies, so i call them,
Don't bother about the heights, Goons and Morons,
Don't care whatever happen to them, Only they know,
how to achieve success,
How to defeat the fear, fear of failure and death, Because
they know,
If they move back,
The whole queue, full of adrenaline behind them,
Definitely will kneel and give up in a jiffy.

Alas! Many loss precious lives,but Many proves being
heroic,
And so are they idolized.

Raise.

High dreamsIn my eyes, Try they to blind me,
By their atrocities.
They try to handcuff me, So I won't write, Revolutionary
words,
They even try to chop my legs, I won't walk in protests,
Against them,
Even they try to shut my mouth,
"Bol ki lab azad hain tere" won't work afterwards. But,
Alas! They are so ignorant,
They don't know,
My heart and soul is buried, In the soil of my homeland,
My eyes long for her charm , For my people and home,
If I need to die, I am ready,
Let me die, now for her.

<u>Yusra khan</u>

This is Dr. Yusra Khan From Peshwar, Pakistan. I'm a learner, a doctor and a writer, i love literature and arts, find my home here, posting my write-ups wasn't my thing years back but few chapters of my life made me to pour out my thoughts, imaginations onto pieces of paper and here my ink bleed now with purest of my emotions and scars. Always wanted to be a published writer and here i got a chance with forever shinings to shine like a star with my art. Hope you'll find your emotions here in the pool of my write-ups.

<u>"QUOTATIONS"</u>

If you don't do something stupid when you're young than
you don't remember something funny when you get old!

Haters gonna hate,
But you my darling don't loose your worth and shine.

I'm no good without you, come and heal me.

Do you know!
What is your biggest achievement, believing you and not
others.

Don't fall when you can just fly, Fly wild, Fly with hope,
Fly with your goals kept high,
why fall when you can just fly and dream high, Fly and
don't shy.

You glow differently when You're actually happy.

Not all men are same,
As not all women are downtrodden.

Don't live with the heavy heart, Instead persue purity in
mind.

My new take on life,
Soaking up the positive energy and immersing in life.

"Lady of Magnanimity"

Riding on the boat of Courage and Confidence She's the
Captain of her own ship
She's a sparkle
That many want to Tackle Building up a Strong Empire
That LADY of Aspire
With bricks of Boldness and Bravery With surety of her
AUDACITY
Her journey is Long Haul Surpassing it Daringly and not
Fool Heartedly
The words that merely like Boulders Of those
judgmental group of people
Can't CEASE her doing WELL leaving marks Of
Victory Those jesters making Defamatory statements
Have to Flip-Flopp their Assumptions When they get to
know her
She's a LADY of Fire and Desire
They question about how ATROCIOUS she is? Do I
have to Tell'em
How Intellectual she is! How Fearless she is!
How Independent she is! How Original she is!
Just because she is a woman of, High social position
She's a LADY of thick skin
And Men fear of her Frenziness Lady of Magnanimity
Who stand in front of many

Who isn't alone in her Crucial Journey Because of her
Resolute Character
She became so Appealingso badass. °
_Yishuzahwrites
"Larki he to hun"

Larki he to hun,
Koi gunahgar khatakar to nahi,

Kyun mujhe dunya ki zangeerun me bandh diya jata hai,
Kyun mere masoom se khawabun ko nocha jata hai,
Kyun uski shakhsiyat ko kaala dagh bna dya jata hai,
Kyun meri soch par mera khud ka ikhtyar nahi,
Kyun meri har raah me khnchi jate hy lakeer, Kyun mjhe
be-rung be-boo bna dya jata hai,
Meray hontun ki muskurahat ko cheen lya jata hai, Kyun
bachpan he se mere parrun ko kaat dya jata hai, Keh phr
kbhi unchi uraan he na ur sakun?
Apni ummedun pe khud pura na utrun,
Aur phir jawan hune pe ye boojh kisi aur k kaandhy pe
laad dya jata hai, Nahi samjh mje dunya ki in dallelun ki
rakhni,
Nahi qail ln rasm-o-riwaj ka huna, Nahi kisi fitwey ko
qabool karna,
Kyun me be hun ik qaid parindey ki manand,
Kyun nahi hai ijazat mjhy sirf aur sirf apne dil ko sunney
ki, Kyun nahi hai ijazat mje srf aur srf khud ko sunney
ki,
Me kyun sab ki ummedun pe poora utrun, Kiya mjhe
khud se piyar karne ki ijazat nahi, Kyun khud aitamaadi
ka yahan riwaj nahi,
Han, larki to hun main mgr dunya ke isharun par chalne
wali katputli nae hun me.
_*Yishuzahwrites*

<u>Awaleen</u>

Awaleen is a 23 year old hailing from Srinagar who is currently pursuing masters in journalism

"Splatter of darkness"

I bided this for months .... to finally sit myself and cross
you out from my life wholly. Thought I wouldn't feel
anything if i do so.. but i did a little tho!☺
When my hands reached my lap..
And i had to go down the memory bank. once again,
Which was more convoluted than i can ever imagine,
My heart started running wild..thought i would pass out.
but i had to calm my silly heart
telling it "don't be stupid again, you getting wild is not
worth it" So i came back to myself   and start
Deleting those pictures with my trembling hands
          which each picture i hit delete .
The memories started getting vague
Before my eyes....Each picture of you started echoing
lies, those screenshots of your
Special gist started making fun of itself and they
welcomed barfing scandals,
Betrayals and warning signs that i had stupidly barred
from entering into my league.   but
today i absorbed all your
Wrong doings...and surprisingly I didn't let my precious
diamonds out of my eyes....
It was time to curb them and save for myself   because
my eyes,my soul and every darn
inch of me is valuable and im not going to ever waste it
on some toxic part of my life. 🦋

"The final letter"

 I sensed "An angelic halo"
but u turned into a Demonic darkness. I sensed loyalty...
But you turned into a trickster.
I sensed truthfulness but you turned into A gazillion
pieces of ..lies,
a single Piece was
enough to scar my fairytales   for real.
But i still decided to shroud myself into
The cage of deception for "Four long years"
I could have destroyed the walls you build around.
                   ☺
But I decided to make a massive deal, By suffocating
myself in the kingdom
Of lies.......each day each second i cried you a river.. and
u used my teardrops to sail your
Boat away from me,not alone but with someone
new..leaving me all numb And broken synchronously....
I couldn't brace my self with the worst betrayal that you
presented me with...
But u left me no choice but to live with the Heartache.

Today i broke the "walls of misapprehension "
Turned my tears into a deadly venom...
So If someone tries to swim away in em again....
Their soul will tremble and ask for forgiveness & regret
their doings   to
The eternity   and beyond.
leen

"SHE"•••••~

She is a person of forbearance .. She will keep her
calm...
She is a person of fidelity
She will keep herself in one direction She is a person of
promises
She will never break em She is a person of humility
She will keep her standards alive... She is a person of
royalty
She always keeps her head held high..♛ •••••••••~•
But once you mess up with her self esteem, her
allegiance, She will return as a lethal "WOMAN"
Who wont be afraid to pick herself up
Despite of falling gazillion times and looking even more
stronger than ever!

_Leen

Alfiya Anjum

Lafz alfazon ke sheher me khud ko talash rahe hain,a girl
from hassan, Karnataka

1. Mulakath toh tujhse pehli baar huvithi,
Ajnabi kam aur o kuch apne pann ka ehsaas degaya tu,
mere alfazon ko samjha hi par mery khamoshi ko bhi
samjh gaya tu, un havavon me Mohabbath ki khushboo
bikher gaya tu,
Par mulakhath kuch adhurisy chod gaya tu...

2. Mana un lamhon ko khulke jiya hamne hai,
par akhir me akele rehne ke dar ne daraya bhi toh hame
hai,
A ajeeb sy uljhan hai eak taraf samandar toh dusri taraf
khaayee bhi toh hai, Bus pair fisalneki dery hai aur
marna mukaddar me bhi toh hai.....

3. Jala diya tha kuch kahaniyon ko bus is khatir ki
koi use padh sake na,
par jise sari duniya rakh samjhti rahi tune usy rakh se
mery zindagy ki dastan padhhi lee na...